A long time ago, there lived a young man called Crow. He had no family and no one to look out for him. He was often dirty, and he wore rags. He lived on the outskirts of a small town.

The children of the town were horrible to Crow. They made fun of him because he was different, and because he lived alone. But Crow was a very skilled hunter. He caught many birds, and he traded them for other foods.

One day, while Crow was out hunting in the forest, he walked further than he ever had before. He saw a big flat stone with a rounded stone on top. It looked like a seat, so he sat down on it.

“Would you like to hear a story?” said someone next to him.

Crow nearly jumped out of his skin. He looked around, but there was no one there.

“Who said that?” yelled Crow.

No one replied.

“I must be hearing things,” said Crow to himself. But then he heard it again…

“Shall I tell you a story?”

Crow looked around at the stone he was sitting against. He could just make out a nose, a mouth… It was the stone who had spoken!

"Who are you?" said Crow.

"I am the storytelling stone. I have been here forever," said the stone. "Would you like me to tell you a story?"

“Give me one of the birds you caught, and I will tell you how the Earth came to be,” said the stone.

So Crow laid one of his birds on the flat stone.

The stone told Crow how the land was made, and the sky. As the stone finished one story, he started another.

But as the Sun set, the stone told Crow, "Go home now. Do not tell anyone about me, but come back tomorrow and I will tell you more stories."

Crow went back to the stone the next morning, and the next, each time bringing a bird to hear more tales.

Because Crow was giving so many birds to the storytelling stone, he could not bring as many birds back to the town as he normally did. Soon, the others began to spot this. They assumed that Crow had lost his hunting skills, and the children teased him even more.

“You aren’t even a good hunter,” they said.

One day, Crow came to the stone with another bird offering.

"Storytelling stone, please tell me another story," he said.

But this time the stone said, "You have heard all of the stories I have to tell. Now you must go and tell my stories to others."

So Crow became the first storyteller. He went from town to town, telling the stories that he had heard. Everyone was happy to listen to the stories. They fed Crow and gave him things in return for telling the stories.

One day, Crow turned up at a new town. He told his stories to the whole town. A girl was sitting next to him. She listened to everything Crow had to say. Crow stayed in the town for a while, and he married the girl.

Crow and his wife traveled around, telling stories as they went. They became rich and they wore fine cloaks.

One day, Crow and his wife went back to the town that Crow was from. No one recognized Crow in his fine cloak, with his elegant wife. The whole town listened to his stories. They listened with their ears and their hearts.

Crow told everyone that they must never forget the stories they had heard.

"Tell these stories to your children and grandchildren," he told them.

And so the stories were told, and told, and they are still being told today!